Simon & Schuster Books for Young Readers

An imprint of Simon & Schuster Children's Publishing Division

1230 Avenue of the Americas, New York, New York 10020

Typography by Heather Wood

The text for this book is set in Granjon.

The illustrations are rendered in watercolor.

Printed and bound in the United States of America

3   5   7   9   10   8   6   4   2

Library of Congress Cataloging-in-Publication Data

Tudor, Tasha.

The dolls' Christmas / Tasha Tudor.

p.   cm.

Summary: Two dolls celebrate Christmas by giving a party for their friends.

ISBN 0-689-82809-8

[1. Dolls—Fiction. 2. Parties—Fiction. 3. Christmas—Fiction.] I. Title.

PZ7.T8228Dm 1999   [Fic]—dc21   98-45685

The
DOLLS' CHRISTMAS

TASHA TUDOR

SIMON & SCHUSTER BOOKS FOR YOUNG READERS

I HAVE A SPECIAL FONDNESS FOR THIS BOOK. For many years, my family and I celebrated our own dolls' Christmas, and it became a holiday tradition we all cherished.

My fascination for dolls and dollhouses began when I was seven years old and my mother made me a dollhouse for Christmas. We named it "Pumpkin House" because it was magical, just like the pumpkin in the Cinderella tale. I believed in that magic all through my childhood years.

Later, as a young mother, I needed something to keep my children busy while I prepared Christmas dinner and decorated the tree. To have the dolls celebrate Christmas seemed like the perfect diversion. As the children got older, it became much more elaborate, evolving into a large celebration with their friends, dolls, and stuffed animals. Before long the

whole family got involved, and the dolls' marionette show became a project everyone enjoyed working on.

The dollhouse was quite real to all of us. By celebrating the dolls' Christmas, we were able to enjoy Christmas twice. My children learned the very essence of giving as they made gifts for the dolls to give to each other. Eventually, the dolls came to epitomize the spirit of goodwill, both for me and my children.

It was all great fun and those memories are among my happiest. The Tudor dolls continue to celebrate Christmas even though my children now have children of their own. Magic isn't meant to be limited to childhood. If properly nourished, it will last a lifetime.

— *Tasha Tudor*

ONCE UPON A TIME there were two very old dolls who lived with two little girls in an old red house. The dolls' names were Sethany Ann and Nicey Melinda. The girls' names were Laura and Efner.

Sethany Ann was French and very elegant. Nicey Melinda wasn't elegant but she was full of character. She had the brightest eyes of blue glass and a nose quite worn down from generations of loving and scrubbing.

The dolls were extremely fortunate for they had a house all their own, which was named Pumpkin House.

Sethany and Nicey were not dollhouse dolls at all; they were large dolls, over a foot tall. What was so wonderful about Pumpkin House was that it was the right size for large dolls. It took up the side of a room and even turned the corner. Efner had to stand on a chair to reach the second floor. Pumpkin House had a kitchen, two bedrooms, a bathroom, a parlor, a dining room, a front hall, a conservatory with real pots of plants, and a live turtle named Ezekiel. The house had everything two dolls could need, from an iron stove in the kitchen to a complete set of china in the dining-room cupboards. It even had electric lights and a handsome horsehair sofa.

Every year at Christmas, Sethany and Nicey had a dinner party and a Christmas tree of their own, and after dinner they had a marionette show given especially in their honor, to which they invited all their friends. Laura and Efner sent out the invitations on doll-size notepaper by Sparrow Post.

This is what the invitation said:

Miss Sethany Ann
and
Miss Nicey Melinda
request the pleasure of your company
at a
Marionette Show
on Christmas Day
at Candlelight
at the Red House

Of course there had to be a great deal of preparation for such a party. Two days before the party Laura and Efner dressed Nicey and Sethany in their warmest clothes and took them to the woods to get the dolls' Christmas tree.

When they came home they had tea to warm themselves and then decorated the tree with silver nutmegs and golden pears and bright balls of many colors. They made a paper chain and cornucopias and wound the tree round and round with tinsel.

The day after gathering greens the children's cousins arrived for the holidays. One of the cousins had a doll named Lucy, who was Sethany's and Nicey's best friend. She was taken to the spare room of Pumpkin House, where she and Nicey and Sethany spent a happy morning talking about many things. Dolls do talk, you know.

In the afternoon the dolls put on their aprons and came to the kitchen to help with the party preparations. There were cookies to be cut with thimbles, small pies to be rolled, a pan of tiny biscuits and a small mold of jelly to be made. The dolls felt quite tired when everything was finally finished and put away. They went to bed in expectation of tomorrow.

The dolls awoke to find three stockings hanging on the mantelpiece. They were filled with tiny presents and topped off with doll-size candy canes.

After opening their stockings the dolls spent the day quietly until four, when they were washed, powdered, and dressed in their best clothes. Laura cut a bouquet of rose geraniums for Sethany to hold and pinned some in her hair, too. The dolls looked very beautiful.

Lucy, Nicey, and Sethany came downstairs as the tall clock struck half past three. Dinner was to be served in the parlor of the red house because there wasn't room in Pumpkin House for all the guests. Just three dolls had been invited, as the dinner service was for six only. Their names were Henrietta, Meg, and Trilby, and they were waiting in the hall. All the dolls went in to dinner.

What a delightful sight met their eyes! On one side of the room stood the dolls' tree, completely surrounded by presents. In the middle of the room was the bread-board, spread with a lacy cloth. There were four candles in silver candlesticks and a centerpiece of geraniums and parsley. Tiny place cards told them where to sit. The boys of the family played butler and served the dinner.

There were three courses beginning with soup and ending with ice cream and champagne in a doll-size bottle, only it was ginger ale. They all enjoyed themselves immensely.

After dinner the dolls sat about the tree and opened their presents. I couldn't possibly tell you all that they received, for that would take too long. By candlelighttime all was in readiness for the marionette show. The family was dressed in old-fashioned clothes. The children and dolls sat waiting for their guests.

The first to arrive were Tedward and Edward Bear, Effilly Elephant, Trilby, and Mr. Kitty. Then came Lily, Oliver Twist, Meg, Henrietta, and several others.

When everyone was assembled the candles were blown out and the play *Little Red Riding Hood* began.

Everyone had the best time, at least everyone but Trilby, who was sat upon for half the performance, and Mr. Kitty, who fell to the floor in a fright at the sight of the wicked wolf. When the play was over they ate cookies and the children sang carols around the big Christmas tree. Then the guests went home, all but Effilly, who was forgotten. He spent the night under the table and had an interesting discussion with some mice about cake crumbs compared to peanuts.

In Pumpkin House the dolls went to bed. "I think," said Nicey, "that Christmas is the most magic time of all the year, not just for the pretty things you get, but for the feeling inside you of what a good place the world is to live in. I should know, for I have seen one hundred and ten Christmases!"